I dedicate the story of *The Mermaid Princess* to my husband, Eric Cua! We've been on a journey together over the course of the past 18 years and Eric has always dared me to dream, encouraged me, and believed in me. He's made sure my dreams become my reality, and for that I am forever grateful!

www.mascotbooks.com

The Mermaid Princess

©2017 Jennifer Cua. All Rights Reserved. No part of this publication may be reproduced, stored in a retrieval system or transmitted in any form by any means electronic, mechanical, or photocopying, recording or otherwise without the permission of the author.

For more information, please contact:
Mascot Books
560 Herndon Parkway #120
Herndon, VA 20170
info@mascotbooks.com

Library of Congress Control Number: 2017902528

CPSIA Code: PRT0517A
ISBN-13: 978-1-68401-283-1

Printed in the United States

The Mermaid Princess

Written By: Jennifer Cua

Illustrated By: Lonai Leach

Once upon a time, in the deep blue sea,
lived a mermaid princess named Lorelea!

She was beautiful inside and out,
and the creatures of the ocean loved her without a doubt.

Lorelea was a princess who sought out adventure and fun,
swimming all day long in the ocean sun.

Her tail glitzed and glowed as she swam about,
her confidence beaming without a doubt.

She wondered what it would be like to encounter the terrifying legend of the sea,

a sea dragon as awful and dreaded as could be.

Truth be told,

he was both crabby and old!

Lorelea's parents often warned her of the dangers in the sea, but none of their warnings seemed to worry Lorelea!

One day Lorelea decided to wander from home,
coming upon treasure that seemed mysteriously unknown!

She contemplated what to do, and as she floated away, she heard a voice call out, "Hey!"

She looked behind her and was surprised to see
a great sea dragon that appeared angry!

"Oh no!" she gasped as she froze in place,
hoping the dragon would not pursue her in a chase.

In a flash, Lorelea thought, *I need to take a stand!*
And it came upon her to offer the dragon her hand!

The dragon looked at her with confusion in his eyes.
Who was this mermaid? What a surprise!

He had planned to act fierce and mean
and scare the mermaid until she swam away with a scream!

But he extended his scaly hand too,
and he and Lorelea bonded as friends anew.

In fact, they were friends and happy to be,
as the sea dragon had been very lonely!

The sea dragon was simply misunderstood,
and it became Lorelea's mission to help him do good.

With her help, he made lots of new friends,
and her family adopted him in the end.

He was accepted and loved all around,
the nicest sea dragon ever to be found!

They all lived happily ever after in the Deep Blue Sea,
swimming together in perfect harmony!

The moral of the story, as Lorelea would say,
is something she learned on that fateful day.

Be kind to all creatures unique or alike,
and your heart will be filled with laughter and delight!

About the Author

Jennifer was born and raised in North Canton, Ohio. She attended college at Kent State University and studied Early Childhood Education. It was her dream to teach young children and she achieved this dream after graduating college when she relocated to Raleigh, North Carolina, to teach first grade!

Jennifer still resides in the Raleigh area with her husband and two children. After having children of her own, she shifted gears and began a career in a directing role of childcare facilities, affording her the opportunity to remain career-oriented while still spending time with her son and daughter throughout the day. In addition to her love of young children and early learning, Jennifer is an avid dog lover and rescuer. Her family participates in dog foster programs on top of having four large dogs of their own! Labs have always held a special place in her heart and she has recently found a love for Great Pyrenees.

Jennifer has always had a passion for early learning and literacy. She loves children's books and writing, and hopes her books will allow families to come together and enjoy story time for years to come!